FORBIDDEN ECSTASY

Secret lovers in a secret world

Daniel Elijah Sanderfer

JUNE 1, 2019

TABLE OF CONTENTS

THE NEW REVEREND

The sun glistened off the picturesque meadow in the hot Indiana summer sun. Noah was helping his father at the wood shop, but his mind was distracted. He would rather be out playing in the creek or anywhere but this hot sweatshop of a saw house.

"Noah," His father yelled from across the room, "Where is your mind at today, we got to get this order out for the new reverend and his son. They can't move into a house without any furniture."

Noah had been working with his dad ever since he could remember. Their family sustained off his mother's sewing, alteration repairs and his father's saw shop. His dad could take a tree and turn it into any piece of beautiful furniture anyone could want. They had been busy for the past month on a big order that could support the family for a year. A wealthy outsider was moving into town, and it was all anyone could speak.

The town of Elizabeth Indiana never saw much action. They had a small gas station, a school, and that was about it. If you needed something special, you had to drive thirty minutes into town. New Albany was like New York to the kids of Elizabeth, with its fancy stores and restaurants. Any boy on summer break could find himself in a lot of trouble if he wanted to there.

At eighteen, Noah was ready; he spent his whole life as a good boy being a part of Amish society there wasn't a choice unless you wanted to get shunned. He could not imagine life without being able to speak to his family. They were all he had ever known-he turned his attention to the freshly cut boards coming down the saw; it was his job to catch them as his father pushed them through.

Noah was tall and lanky with an athletic build from being a hard-working farm boy; he had hair as red as a summer rose and a body pale as winter snow. His arms and face were rosy from working outside all the time. He also had a wispy beard starting. It was cute; all the other boys had full-grown beards. Whereas he just had a few noticeable chin hairs, and they were red just like his hair. His body had just come into its own after being a smaller child. His muscles and abs were developing perfectly. To put it politely, he was a very handsome boy.

His dad was the opposite. He was short and very tan- with skin tougher than leather. The hot summer sun had practically baked him over the years. He had dark hair with a perfectly manicured Amish beard. He was quite handsome, even at fifty his wife Rachel always smiled with pride, knowing she had married such a handsome man. When he was younger, he had helped his father put tin roofs on houses and do miscellaneous gardening.

It was an old-fashioned life and a world very different from the one just thirty minutes away. Their little community thrived well. Everyone sustained off the land and by helping one another. Every Sunday, they were in church, followed by large family gatherings with delicious things to eat. The women would slave away for hours in the kitchen as the menfolk talked on the front porch about hunting and farming. Most of the boys on Sunday could be found at the creek swimming, while the girls helped their mothers prepare dinner.

Noah's mom Rachel was the ringleader of the ladies. She was a very outspoken woman with a temper like fire. The men often reprimanded her for speaking her opinion when not asked, but that's why Zeb loved her.

She was beautiful. Over six feet tall with a slender body and ample bosom that left little for modesty. Her hair was beautifully red like Noah's; in fact, she is where he got his looks. Had it not been for the midwife and his father being there for the delivery. It was hard to tell Zeb and Noah were related at all.

Rachel loved to cook and the summer; she would often open the kitchen windows to the farmhouse and let the warm air traipsing across the meadow fill the whole house with light and warmth. They had so much to be thankful for; their farm had a bump of the crop this year, which meant busy canning work, but she would have enough for the whole winter.

They also had an assortment of livestock, which she had named all of them lovingly. It was one of the hardest parts of farm living. She grew so attached to every little creature on the farm. When harvest time came, she would often have trouble killing them. It was part of life, though; she would thank God for their service. The only comfort she felt was knowing they were serving her family. Zeb had let her keep a few animals as pets, but most people from Mennonite society found material things unnecessary; he bent the rules for her so that she could be happy.

She came from a more progressive family further north and was raised in what conservative Amish families referred to as "*Gay churches,*" where the women would dress in regular dresses instead of the handmade garb of their own toiling. She maintained her position in this more conservative community by wearing what was required when out amongst fellow community members. At home, she was just Rachel, in her pretty flowy dresses often adorned with flowers.

Her husband Zeb loved her free-thinking spirit so much. She reminded him of the beautiful girls he had seen in Louisville, where he went for Rumspringa many years ago. They were outspoken and wore makeup. They just looked so pretty. They were independent with no strings holding them back. At that time, he had thought he would end up leaving the community to marry outside, but shortly after returning, he met Rachel.

He had gone to the gas station to pick up a few things. At the time he was living with his elderly father who could not get out anymore. His mother had passed away many years prior from Pneumonia. She was with her family, and he had accidentally bumped into her in the store.

She shouted at him, "Watch where you're going," and angrily slapped his arm.

Her parents had quickly apologized and sent her back to the truck. When he passed her by, he tipped his hat in a friendly gesture. She responded by sticking her tongue out at him. He knew from that moment; she was the one for him. Beautiful, defiant, and sassy. After a brief courtship, they would marry at the little church, and she would be with child: their only one, Noah.

Rachel called from the porch, "Supper's ready, whenever you all want to quit jaw jacking out here and come to eat."

Zeb shot her a look of offense. She often ignored it. He loved teasing her even after all these years.

She shouted again across the meadow, "Noah James, Dinner!"

The boy lazily strolled through the tall grass. His pants were wet at the bottom where he had been at the creek, wading in the water. His shirt was unbuttoned, showing off his smooth body and physique. Rachel placed her hands on her hips as the boy got closer to the house and quipped, "Where have you been, you are a mess; get changed for dinner, you ain't coming to my table looking like that."

She smiled after scolding him. He entered the large farmhouse and dropped his shoes in the entryway. His father shouted, "Afternoon, Son, how's the water today?"

Noah grinned, "Perfect, It is warm, and with the rain, last night, up a little bit."

Zeb smiled as he took his seat at the head of the table. Noah was something else, just like his mother; he did what he wanted to, never thinking about the repercussions from the decisions he made. He would decide to do something and then get on with it.

Rachel had gone back to the kitchen with the other ladies to get everything ready to serve. They were like an assembly line. One would prepare the plates; another would cut the meat, another would serve. She yelled at Noah, who was washing up in the downstairs water closet, "Hurry up, The new reverend and his son will be here any minute for dinner."

Noah rolled his eyes in protest. He would much rather take his dinner to his room and be alone with his thoughts, than socializing with strangers. He changed into some black trousers his mother had made. They were very sharp and appropriate for the pastoral company. He also threw on an old flannel shirt his father had purchased from the tractor supply store in town. He loved that shirt; it was green like his eyes, and it fit in all the right places, showing off his muscular frame and chiseled features.

He hastily tucked it in and slid on his church shoes. Not the most coordinated outfit, but he was a young man and paid little attention to detail. He was more concerned with dinner at this point. After a day of running around with friends, he was famished. He walked into the dining room to show his father his outfit for approval.

His dad smiled, "What about that hair?"

Noah pushed it down with his hands, but it was frizzy, and after being in the sun, it was as copper toned as a new penny, and there was no remedy to tame it in such a short period of time.

"That'll do son," his father said with a grin.

A knock at the door interrupted the inspection, prompting Rachel to yell, " Will someone get that?"

Noah sprinted to the door like a shot from a rifle; he knew better than to let someone knock twice. As he passed his father, Zeb said, "Probably the new pastor and his son."

Noah flung the door open a little faster than intended. He always liked the potential of having another boy his age to hang out with. It was hard to find ones that carried the same interests as him. So often their differences would prove to be too much of a challenge to work around, and they would grow apart. But he was feeling very optimistic about a minister's son.

He was quiet and reserved; he often liked to daydream. He was a hard worker and would remain silent during work days. He had heard this new pastor came from one of the large churches in the city; he was fascinated with that culture, and he had often wished his community were more progressive and did not have so many rules. Maybe things would change now? The tall skinny man smiled and shot out a hand to shake Noah's, "Hello, young man!"

Noah took his hand and mumbled, "Hi, you must be the new reverend."

The man replied joyfully, "Why yes, sir, that is I. Oh, and this is my son, Jerimiah."

The pastor stepped to the side. Noah stood at the door in silence; he felt his heart flip-flop. The boy was striking. He was tall with wavy dark brown hair. Muscular with a very strong body built like a house. He extended his hand to Noah. He had big soft manly hands and a grip that could crush walnuts, with a wink and smile he said, "Hello bud, I'm Jeremiah."

He had a deep sensual voice, and as he spoke, Noah closed his eyes; he could feel the syllables of the boy's words reverberating into his soul. His voice soothed and enchanted him. Dare he look into this striking young man's eyes?

As he did, Jerimiah met his gaze; he noticed they were naturally sleepy looking, in a sensual way. They were brown and deep with a strong, reserved feel. Noah wasn't sure what he was feeling, but it was euphoric, and as they stood staring at one another it felt like two mirrors gazing into infinity with no pre-determined destination; all there was, was this moment, and he never wanted it to end. As Noah snapped back into reality, he motioned the reverend and Jerimiah to come inside. He apologized for the delay, and the kind reverend responded with a smile, "Quite alright young man, you're a thinker, and I like that."

As Jeremiah stepped inside the farmhouse, Noah could not help but notice Jerimiah's body; his tucked in flannel shirt was sticking to his hard abs, leaving nothing to the imagination, and all Noah could think about was how he would give anything to be that shirt, wrapped like a second skin around Jerimiah body.

He was also wearing tight blue jeans with a belt. The buckle was huge, and Noah felt his eyes drift further south. He took note of Jerimiah's beautifully proportionate body and a tight muscular butt that left him wondering how he got it all in a pair of jeans so tight. Jeremiah glanced Noah's direction and caught him checking him out. He smiled to himself at the attention he had commanded from the quiet young guy.

He always saw himself as older mentally than normal boys his age. He was only twenty himself but had a very mature presence. As they greeted Zeb and Rachel, he asked Noah, "So, have you guys always been here on the farm?"

Noah was nervous; he found he could barely speak to Jerimiah without getting flustered. "Yes, sir," he squeaked, "I was born and raised right here on the farm," Clearing his throat he continued, "Hey, maybe I can show you around while you are here?"

"That would be great," Jeremiah replied, excitedly.

Suddenly, Rachel and the other women emerged with all the fruit of their labor from cooking. They were all seated at the big dining table as Zeb asked the good Reverend about where he was from. The man was joyous and well educated. He had left his original community after Rumspringa and married a young woman who was not from the Amish community. He explained, "I had a rebellious streak when I was younger. I found myself needing more than what I had seen in my adolescence."

Rachel was fascinated with his story. She had somehow managed to be a trailblazer for Amish woman. Speaking out of turn and offering her wisdom and advice on things. She believed that God was a loving God and not one of anger, which was very taboo for someone in her community to believe, especially forming an opinion of her own like that. She asked the pastor, "So where is your wife?"

The reverend's face washed with sadness, "She, unfortunately, went to be with the Lord after an illness, she had contracted pneumonia and just could not recover."

It saddened Rachel. She exclaimed, "That is so terrible, I am sorry you had to experience that pastor."

He smiled at her, "Quite all right, my dear, she is a lot better with the Lord than in this wicked old world."

Zeb added, "Bless you, sir; it takes a strong person to recover from something that tragic."

The boys had just finished dinner and asked if they could be excused. They didn't wait for their fathers to answer.

"Where are you all off to," Zeb said with an inquisitive tone.

Noah replied meekly, "I just wanted to show Jeremiah the creek and the animals if that is okay with you and the reverend?"

"That will be just fine," Zeb nodded.

The reverend added, "Be back before dark."

Rachel scowled at them, "Yes, you best be back to wash up before bed. Your chores start early in the morning."

Noah didn't hear her; he was in a hurry, and he had high hopes that he may have found a friend in Jeremiah, but only time would tell. They bolted from the house and out into the field. The wind swept across it, and the smell of fresh summer rain was in the air. The sun was sweeping lower in the sky as they made it to the creek.

Jeremiah called out, "This place is beautiful," as he spun around with a look of wonder on his face; trying to capture the scenic image in his mind. He mumbled, "So much better than the city."

Noah turned to reply, "You have seen the city?"

"I sure have," Jerimiah replied while untying his shoes, then he continued, "It's very busy with many different kinds of people."

Noah closed his eyes, trying to envision it; he longed to be around other people like himself, who enjoyed thinking and writing. While Noah was lost in his thoughts, Jeremiah had already stripped off his jeans and shirt. He was wearing nothing but his briefs as he jumped into the creek. Noah turned and saw the boy's clothes on the creek bank. Jerimiah emerged, pushing his soaked brown hair back; he sighed with pleasure, "Oh, that feels so good!"

Jerimiah was such a beautiful man; he moved to the edge, reaching up to pull Noah in too. Noah protested, "Mama will kill me if I get wet in these clothes."

He lost his balance and fell in; Jeremiah catching him. As he resurfaced to the top, his clothes were stuck to his body.

Jeremiah laughed as Noah struggled to gain his footing. He offered the boy a hand to help him up, and Suddenly, they found their bodies pressed tightly against one anothers. Jeremiah's arms around his waist, holding him up. The last rays of sunshine were reflecting off the surface of the cool water. All was quiet and still. They were face to face, and Noah did not know what he was feeling inside, but he did know it was nice being so close to him. He pulled away quickly at the sound of his mother Rachel yelling across the meadow. "Boys, it's getting dark; come home now!"

They froze for a moment gazing at each other, wet and cold there in the water; Jerimiah, in his underwear and Noah's clothes leaving little to the imagination. It was like they were exploring one another as men. Noticing the details of each other's physique. They could feel one another's chest expand as they breathed. They were one with each other and with nature. Noah pulled away quickly and climbed up the bank, while Jeremiah breathlessly watched him for a moment longer before jumping up after him.

Noah cried, "Hurry up; we are going to be in big trouble."

Jeremiah replied unconcerned, "We will be fine."

He tucked his shirt back in although his dry clothes were like a sponge on his body, Soaking in all the water. They sprinted across the meadow back to the farmhouse. Noah was feeling so anxious; he did not know how he would explain them being wet, and in his good clothes too.

Running across the golden field, golden sunlight flashed in between the shadows of their bodies. When they got back to the farmhouse Zeb, and the Pastor were chatting about crops and how well they were doing this year. Rachel looked worried, she scowled at them as they stepped up on the front step, drenched and out of breath.

She scolded Noah, "Where have you been; you are soaking wet, you better not have gone swimming!"

Noah glanced away, chastised. Jeremiah spoke up, in his defense "Were sorry Ma'am, Noah was showing me the beautiful creek, and I got too close, when I fell in, he was just trying to help and fell in too."

Her expression softened, but only a little. Noah watched the boy in shock for protecting him. He knew he would be in big trouble, and there were going to be heavy chores and punishment for pulling a stunt like this. Jeremiah turned to him and winked. Noah smiled back, his soul melting inside like a candle in the night. The reverend laughed and commented on the two, "Well, boys will be boys!"

Zeb laughed at the comment, "That is true."

Rachel frowned at the two men for making light of it, and quipped, "Go inside a get dried off now; you must be getting to bed soon, chores don't wait for late risers in the morning."

Jeremiah spoke up again, asking Noah's parents and his father, "Can we come back tomorrow?"

The Reverend replied, "Well, we sure can. We have some furniture to pick up from these gentlemen for the parsonage."

Jeremiah smiled at Noah, and Noah smiled back at him. "See you tomorrow then," Noah said excitedly.

Jeremiah replied, "Yes sir," and they shook hands before Rachel rushed Noah inside to get him dried off from their little swimming trip. The Reverend and Jeremiah hopped in their old pickup and drove to the home they would live in while they were in town.

Minister Zigafoos had served the community for over fifty years when the town people chose him in his early thirties to be their minister. He lived a full life helping the town people through moral dilemmas and tending to the church and parsonage. He was 80 when the Lord called him home in his sleep.

He was discovered when one of the local farmers stopped by to bring him a lunch plate from his wife. They worried about him, he was very fragile, and with him being all alone out there, they wanted to make sure he did not fall or get hurt. He meant a great deal to the community; just like a grandfather to them all, and when the news of his passing hit. They were all devastated.

Settling In 🏠

The Reverend pulled up to the old wooden church located on the outskirts of town. It was a ramshackle little building whose paint job was cracking and baked from the hot sun. Behind it was a small cottage. It was wooden and painted white. It had unique handmade shutters and an old rusty metal roof. A large front porch and behind it was a meadow that was overgrown where in his younger days the minister would garden. The good reverend looked over to his son Jeremiah, "Well, buddy, we have got a lot of work to do!"

Jeremiah sighed. It was nothing like he had pictured. He missed their cabin close to the city and their nice newer church building; fixing this place up was going to take all summer. The man smiled at the boys less than enthusiastic expression.

He tousled Jeremiah's hair, "It will be okay son. We will have this place whipped into shape in no time."

Jeremiah opened the truck door and stepped out onto the dirt lot, accommodating as the church parking lot. It was dark now, and the air was brisk. He could hear it whistling through the pine trees. Occasionally, he could hear wildlife, like the owls calling out into the night. He was a little taken back, and he was not one to scare easy. His dad jumped out and closed the truck door behind him; his abrupt tone caused Jeremiah to jump, "We better get some lights on and see what we are working with."

Jeremiah didn't say it, but he thought that was an excellent idea. He wanted to get inside as quickly as possible. They opened the door to the little cottage that was the church parsonage. It squelched out across the meadow like an animal that had been captured. The home thankfully had electricity. They only used it when necessary though. Jeremiah crowded his dad, and the light flickered on. The good reverend was always a very positive man; he exclaimed: "Well, this isn't bad at all." Jeremiah was in shock.

It was very dirty inside with lots of old letters and paperwork stacked everywhere, notes from the good minister's sermons. Minister Sigafoos was not a very clean man. He lived very simply in his later years, and with him not being able to get around so well, cleaning took second place to anything else.

The Reverend spoke to Jeremiah, trying to comfort him. He could see the look of disgust on the boy's face, "We will get some help cleaning tomorrow from that dear Rachel and the ladies in the community, let's find the beds to get some rest."

Jeremiah ran outside to get their suitcases from the pickup. The Bishop moved a few stacks of paper off the kitchen table and stacked them neatly on the old desk in the corner of the living room. Jeremiah sat the suitcases down and quipped, "Dad, where are the bedrooms?"

"Well, son, they must be back there." He pointed towards a hallway that split in two directions.

Jeremiah shuddered at the thought of going down there. The walls were dark and covered in smoke from the oil lamps and wood stove. He slowly started walking that way- the old hardwood floors creaking ominously with each step he took. He flicked on the hallway light as he passed the switch. He didn't feel as bad now that there was a little light. Slowly, he turned the doorknob to one of the rooms and opened the door; he was prepared in the event something came jumping out at him, since the house appeared to have not been lived in a while.

It was a cozy little room with a simple wooden bed and nightstand. An oil lamp and bible were sitting on it. Set up for a guest in town. The minister was a wonderful host and very hospitable. Jeremiah was exhausted. He was relieved that the bedroom was at least tidy.

There was a small set of sheets and a beautiful quilt at the foot of the bed. It had been laundered, and he could smell the fresh outdoor air on it as he held it to his face. He loved simple things like that; Fresh laundry, or a quiet rainy evening. As he inhaled the aroma of the clean linen, his mind went back to Noah. It was the same intoxicating smell he had experienced when they were together earlier in the meadow by the creek.

He had always felt different; he had not had the chance to figure out why. The girls in the communities they visited would always flock around him. They were all very polite and nice, wanting to tend to his every need. He found it all uncomfortable. He was old enough now that in his society, he should be settling down, but he was a loner. Strong-willed and carefree. He liked to explore and laugh and get into mischief.

His happiest moments were exploring the woods and tending to garden work, being one with nature; his soul needed it, he didn't have time for frivolous things like chatting with kids or figuring out why the girls would not leave him alone. To him, they were just disturbing his peace.

He was making the bed when his father emerged in the doorway, "Thank goodness they cleaned and made that bed in the old minister's room; I was not too happy about sleeping where the good man passed."

Jeremiah laughed and shook his head. "I imagine not Dad, I know I would not have wanted to either."

The man bid the boy goodnight and slowly closed the door behind him. Jeremiah was in a hurry to strip out of the damp clothes he had been stuck wearing since they left Noah's. He took them all off and opened his suitcase. After toweling off, He tossed on a pair of shorts and a sleeveless shirt he loved. They were comfortable and kept him cool, especially in the small towns that had no air conditioning.

Tonight, was no different; it must have been one hundred degrees outside. He opened the window, and a small breeze wafted in from outside. It was a minor relief, and Jeremiah was thankful. He could not wait to see Noah again tomorrow; he felt drawn to him like a father figure. Noah was quiet and seemed like he needed a friend, and as he drifted into sleep, he kept praying and fantasizing, the cute boy would show up at his window. Jeremiah was a hopeless romantic.

His dad was in the next room, getting ready for bed as well; he always had his rituals of changing into pajamas and saying his prayers. Tonight was the same; he asked the Lord for guidance while they were in town that the people would be open-minded to his different ways. Some towns were less than welcoming to a single father from a big city. His journey in life had made him humble and accepting of a lot of things in life. Even when Jeremiah had told him, he had no desire to settle down with a girl. In fact, He liked boys the way he was supposed to like girls.

His mind drifted back to the night Jeremiah revealed this secret to him. They had been in a small community just like the one they were in now. They had been there for a few weeks, and it was the towns annual harvest festival. Jeremiah had disappeared shortly after church service, and when the reverend had gone to search for him; he found Jeremiah kissing another boy behind the old barn behind the parsonage.

He was angry at the time. Their culture had always instilled this as just lust. With his wife passing away long ago, he could not imagine facing the rest of his life alone. The thought of shunning his only flesh and blood seemed wrong to him. It was as if the Lord would rather have him forgive the boy and accept him for who he was than throw him away.

No, David was not like that. He was a good man, and although he did not understand for sure whether his boy's feelings were acceptable; he knew shunning his only son was not. He encouraged his son to flatter the young girls in the communities when they doted on him and not lead any other boys into temptation. Jeremiah did just that; he knew society was not as kind in these communities as his father had been.

David had promised the first boy Jeremiah had been caught with anonymity. Neither he or Jeremiah would reveal to the boy's parents what they had been doing. At twenty though, he could not hold back the boy any longer, any decision Jeremiah made was now his own. He had provided him with the very best knowledge he could in making decisions, and he was confident the boy would find his way. It was nice having him there for support too; his life was lonely enough without the thought of losing his son also.

His First Time

The next morning, David was up early as usual; he liked to spend his mornings with God and collecting his thoughts for the day. He was a very coordinated man and liked to start the day with a plan; he would always try to get as much good as he could manage done that day.

Jeremiah was still sleeping when his father came to wake him; his dreams had been filled with sweet Noah all night, and he could not wait to see him.

David knocked, "Son, it's time to wake up; we have a lot to do today."

He groaned in response and rolled over, tossing his pillow over his head, hoping his father would somehow forget. No luck though, as his father announced his entrance and came right in, "Up and at em' boy, we have to get this place into shape. I am hoping Zeb's wife Rachel can round up the ladies and help get some of the old reverend's things packed up."

Jeremiah yawned and stretched, finally sitting himself up in the bed. He scooted to the side and sat for a moment before glancing over to his father, to see why he was still there; he mumbled, "A little privacy, Dad?"

David hopped up and replied, "Oh yeah, sure."

Jeremiah watched him slowly leave the room, closing the door behind him.

He walked lazily over to his suitcase to get a pair of clean jeans and a flannel button-up shirt. He did not want to wear anything too nice; he knew he would be working like a dog all day today, the one highlight was that maybe he would get to spend some more time with his new-found friend.

■■■■■■■■■■■■■■■■■■■■■■■■■■■■■■■■■■■■

Meanwhile, Noah and his father were already finishing breakfast and preparing for work at the shop today. They had everything ready for the good reverend, but there was always work to do. If it was not wood shop work, it was gardening or other chores.

Zeb called from the front door after putting on his hat, "Let's go, boy; the pastor will be here soon to pick up that order."

Noah scurried through the dining room after kissing his mother goodbye for the day.

She called to them, "You all be careful," as they started up the hill to the woodshop.

She had lots of work to do herself. She had breakfast dishes, Clothes to wash, and animals to feed.

Noah ran quickly ahead of his father; he was eager to get a start on the day. It was a bright, beautiful summer day. The wind was lightly blowing the wheat in the fields, and the sun was shining brightly. His father walked up behind him, placing his hands-on Noah's shoulders, "You sure have a spring in your step today, boy; what has got into you?"

Noah smiled, "Nothing Pop, I am well rested and have a lot of energy to spare."

Zeb replied skeptically, "You are just hoping you can run off to the creek with that new friend of yours."

Noah snapped to attention, "That would be nice sir if I can get my work finished, can I?"

His father sighed and shook his head, "We will have to see son."

Noah took his place on the side of the saw, as his father began cutting into a huge log. It had not even been a few minutes, and he was sweating right through his shirt.

Suddenly the men heard a vehicle coming up the driveway to the house. His father paused work for a moment to see who it was, and Noah peered around his father. They didn't know very many people around who had vehicles. Noah lit up, realizing it was the pastor and Jeremiah. He saw them get out of the truck and proceed up to the front door, where Rachel answered. She pointed them toward the direction of the saw shop, and Noah saw Jeremiah running up the hill. He was wearing jeans again and a beautiful orange flannel shirt.

Noah thought, what a beautiful color it was and how it great it looked on Jeremiah's tanned skin. David was slightly out of breath from climbing the little hill up to the shop.

"Hello there, Zeb and Noah," his tone was winded as he spoke.

The gentlemen shouted back a, "Hello," and waved.

"A mighty beautiful day the Lord has blessed us with," Pastor David said with a smile.

Zeb nodded and replied, "It sure is; you gentlemen are out and about early today."

Jeremiah rushed to Noah shaking his hand as he greeted him with a friendly, "Hello."

After some small talk, David continued, "I hope I am not imposing on you, but we could sure use some help in cleaning up the old house. Do you think your dear wife could help us?"

Zeb chuckled, "Well, we sure can see."

The two men made their way back down to the farmhouse to speak with Rachel; leaving Noah and Jeremiah alone momentarily, and Jeremiah could not resist talking to Noah as much as possible, "So, this is where you work?"

Noah nodded as he adjusted a stack of wood, "Yes, I help father with building things, whenever someone orders something."

Jeremiah picked up a hand saw and was observing its sharp teeth. "How do you keep from getting cut?"

Noah grabbed the saw in fear the boy would hurt himself and quipped with a sly grin. "You just have to be careful!"

Jeremiah caught his coy joke and grabbed Noah from behind wrestling him to the ground. Jeremiah could not stand it; Noah looked so beautiful and masculine standing there, his clothing soaked in sweat and clinging to his slender body.

Noah protested, "Hey, we can't horse around here; my father will be back any moment and will be furious if we mess something up."

Jeremiah positioned himself on top of Noah, who was laying on his back, breathing heavy from their struggle. Jeremiah smiled down at him, and Noah smiled back. They were lost for a moment again, observing each-others bodies anxiously awaiting one another's next move.

Noah could feel the pressure of Jeremiah's hips on his and felt himself becoming aroused, so he tossed Jeremiah off to the side and took a knee.

Jeremiah had felt it too, and he quickly tried to direct his mind elsewhere. Thankfully he saw their dad's coming back up to the wood shop. Noah could see that his mother was in her cap and work dress waiting on the porch for his dad to return. She must have agreed to help get the house cleaned up for the Reverend David.

Zeb called Noah's name, and Noah jumped to his feet. "Son, I need to take your mother over to the pastor's house, so she can help get things clean. Can you boys watch the shop while I follow the Reverend to the parsonage?"

David glanced suspiciously at his son Jeremiah; he knew something had been going on, from the way Jeremiah was panting and pulling on the front of his jeans to hide his excitement from playing with Noah. He asked inquisitively, "Will you boys be okay here for a while?"

Jeremiah rose to his feet and replied, "Yes, sir!"

David pursed his lips and added, "You boys behave yourself and be sure to help Noah if he needs it, Jerry."

Jeremiah nodded, and the two men proceeded back down the hill to the driveway. Noah's mother quickly hopped into the truck with his dad, while Jeremiah's father got into his truck and proceeded to guide the way.

Noah turned to address what happened before their dad's interrupted and found Jeremiah staring at him with a mischievous smile, rendering speechless momentarily. His expression looked puzzled as he tried to figure out what was in the devilish boy's mind.

He shouted, "All this horsing around is going to get us in big trouble. My family counts on this business to make a living, and my parents do not condone horseplay!"

Jeremiah shook his head in agreement but did not hear a word Noah said. Noah had begun straightening things up from their wrestling when Jeremiah walked up behind him. He tapped Noah's shoulder, handing him a hand saw that had fallen off one of the tables. As Noah stood to take it from his hand, Jeremiah pulled Noah's body into his, the saw dropping from his hand to the ground.

They stared into each other's eyes. Noah was captivated; it was as if he could see deep into Jeremiah's soul, his sweet, protective nature, his mature experienced ways that were different from his own. He wanted to feel for just a moment what it was like to be him.

Jeremiah knew his dad had warned him to behave, but he could not control his lustful desires any longer; he wanted Noah, and he was going to have him. Their lips met, and Jeremiah wrapped his arm tightly around Noah so he couldn't get away. Noah could feel every muscle in Jeremiah's body tense; he had never kissed another person and was unsure what to do. They stood taking in each other's breath momentarily before slowly separating; their bodies left wanting more than just a kiss.

Noah turned away abruptly, and Jeremiah panicked. "I'm so sorry I don't know what came over me."

Noah replied meekly, "No, I'm sorry. I don't know what's wrong with me. I have wanted to taste you since we first met, but I fear it's a sin."

Jeremiah wrapped his arms around the boy's body from behind and whispered in his ear, "Love of anyone is not a sin. We are just showing love for one another; you are my best friend here."

Noah turned to look into his eyes,
"I've never had a best friend. I don't know
how to be one."

Jeremiah smiled and whispered
sweetly into Noah's ear, "To be a friend one
does not need to know, they just need to be"

Noah turned to face him, and they
stared at one another again for a moment,
their faces edged closer together, and
suddenly, Jeremiah cupped his hand behind
Noah's tilted head. Noah's face lit up with
wonder. Their lips brushed lightly and
remained open just enough, so they could
feel the heat of one another's breath enter in
and out of their bodies. It was as if their
souls were becoming intertwined.

Passion took over, and Jeremiah
began swiftly unbuttoning Noah's shirt as
their tongues playfully flicked one another's
inside their mouths. Once he had revealed
Noah's skin, he placed his hands on the
boy's smooth chest and reeled in the feel of
the softness on his fingertips. Then, he
traveled to the boy's perky nipples. As he
massaged them with his thumbs, Noah's
body shuddered from the intense sensation,
prompting Noah to grip Jeremiah's muscular

arms. All the years of repressed desires were flowing from them like a rushing river, and there was nothing that could stop them.

They separated their lips momentarily, and Noah gasped for air. Jeremiah rested his forehead against his and panted as he asked, "Do you want to see my body too?"

Noah nodded, and slowly began unbuttoned Jeremiah's shirt, each snap that released was like a shot from a gun, causing Jeremiah's body to flinch in anticipation of its reveal. As Noah began to observe the other boys body, he traced his finger across his chest down the lines of his abs to the top of his jeans. Their eyes met, their torsos were inches away from touching. Jeremiah whispered, "Are you sure you want to go further?"

Noah shook his head yes in reply; he couldn't think of a better way to learn about the body than with someone whose body was created just like his, and as Noah placed his hand on the bulge occupying the front of Jerimiah's jeans, he bit down on his bottom lip and gazed curiously into Jeremiah's eyes.

Noah whispered, "Can I open them and touch you there?"

Jeremiah shook his head and whispered, "Yes."

Slowly Noah slid the zipper of the tight jeans down, Jeremiah's boxers instantly popping out the front filled with his cock that was swollen from desire. As Noah snapped the button open, Jeremiah grunted with relief and slid them down a little. He took Noah's hand, cupping it over his erection.

Next, Noah began unbuttoning his own pants, matching the same motion he did with Jeremiah; he reached for Jeremiah's hand, placing it on his erect flesh. Jeremiah was familiar with what to do; He moved his hand slowly down it making Noah's entire body quake with pleasure; he quipped, "What are you doing to me?"

But, Jeremiah didn't stop, not that Noah wanted him to; he was excited to see the amount of pleasure he was making his friend experience, and he replied with a whisper, "I'm massaging you."

Noah observed the action momentarily and extended his hand to touch Jeremiah's matching the boy's motions. Their breathing grew labored, their expression laced with seriousness and determination as they stared deeply into one another's eyes. Noah spoke, breaking the silence, "I feel something rising inside of me."

Jeremiah leaned in to kiss him, and whispered, "Release it, Noah!"

His body began moving to match the rhythm of Jeremiah's hand; he paused and moaned a long breathy sigh as Jeremiah felt his hand become wet with Noah's essence. Moments later, Noah's hand feeling the same sensation of wetness from Jeremiah. He wasn't sure what had happened between them, but he knew it was the most he had ever felt with another human being in his life. He never wanted it to end, and he could not wait for it to happen again. They pressed their foreheads together.

Noah giggled, "You made me wet."

Jeremiah whispered, "Me too."

Jeremiah explained as they pulled their clothes back together, what Noah had experienced was an orgasm. When the body is stimulated in those special parts, it feels a release. Noah grimaced at the details, he didn't mind what his body had done, but he didn't need a thorough explanation. Jeremiah laughed at the face Noah made, and once they had put themselves back together. They kissed one another, and Jeremiah whispered to him, "Now, we are bonded for life."

The boys were not sure how much time had passed, but the moment it seemed to have lasted an eternity.

The boys continued their work conversing with one another; Noah asking Jeremiah questions about city life. They had a surprisingly deep connection with one another and could talk for hours about nothing in particular, the experience they had changed them both. Jeremiah knew one thing was for sure; he loved this boy, and although Noah did not know what to call it yet, he felt the same about him. When their eyes met, they could stare straight into one another's souls and feel the attraction burning between them.

It was getting to be close to noon. Rachel, Zeb, and the minister had been toiling away cleaning and organizing the house all morning while the boy's worked and played. David finally broke the silence, "My goodness, Pastor Sigafoos must have been a knowledgeable man!"

Zeb replied, "He sure was, anytime you saw him; he was writing or reading the bible."

Rachel added, "He was a wonderful man, any problem you had, he always had a wise way to fix it."

David smiled, "I hope I can build that kind of relationship with everyone in town."

Zeb patted the man on the back reassuringly, "Once they get to know you, you will be like family. I hope you're ready to gain some weight, the women folk around here love to feed the pastor."

David patted his small belly. "Speaking of which I could do with some lunch."

Zeb replied, "You know what, that sounds like an excellent idea."

Rachel paused from her scrubbing in the kitchen to wash and dry her hands, "Well, that sounds like a cue to take a break."

They all laughed together and made their way outside to the porch where Rachel addressed the two men, "It just so happens I had a roast in the oven. How about some sandwiches?"

David and Zeb smiled at the kind women, and Zeb replied, "I think that sounds wonderful, the boys are probably famished as well."

Rachel made her way to the truck, and the two men followed. They drove back to the farmhouse to find Jeremiah and Noah sitting on the porch. Jeremiah had his feet propped up on the porch rail with his hat over his eyes. Noah was in the porch swing, starring out into nothing.

When they heard the sounds of the vehicles pull up, Jeremiah peeked out from under his hat. Noah sprung up from his seat to greet them. He made his way down the steps, and his mother stepped out of the truck brushing her apron off. "I'm sure you boys are hungry?"

David called a friendly hello to Jerry, and the boy slowly got up to return his greeting with a lazy, "Hi Dad."

Zeb peered up toward the saw shop and noticed all the neatly stacked boards that had been cut and prepared for future jobs, "You boys have been doing a lot of work I see."

Jeremiah spoke for them, "We sure have sir."

David patted his son on the back. "Good job, son."

Noah smiled at Jerry, and he winked back at the boy. Noah blushed, and his mother went to the front door to unlock it. She turned to address them. "You boys come on in to get cleaned up, and changed for lunch."

Jeremiah replied with a nod, "Yes, Ma'am!"

Noah raced up the stairs to his room, and Jeremiah followed. Noah began tearing his sweaty clothes off, and Jeremiah stood in the doorway, watching him with a smile. Noah caught him looking and smiled back, "What you are you looking at?"

Jeremiah tipped his hat, "Just you."

Noah bit his bottom lip; he was flattered by the attention. Jeremiah entered the room and closed the door behind him. All though Noah was smaller than he was, he wanted to change out of his sweaty sawdust covered shirt. He asked Noah, "Do you have a shirt I can borrow?"

Noah smiled and handed him a dark blue plaid shirt that complimented his eyes well. He then turned to the mirror with a comb trying to tame his copper hair, which was sticking up with frizz from the heat. He also observed Jeremiah changing his clothes in the background, and Jeremiah winked at him.

They both always could seem to feel when the other was watching. Jeremiah peeled the sweaty shirt from his body, and Noah passed him a washcloth from the pitcher and bowl stand in his room. He began rubbing the cool cloth over his neck and chest, little moans of relief escaping from his body as he did. Noah could feel himself rising again.

Before Jeremiah put the shirt on, he held it up to his nose. Taking in the essence of the sunshine and the boy he was in love with. He loved the idea of wearing something that had been on Noah's body. He slipped the shirt on and buttoned it up when Noah turned around to see how it looked on him. He noticed it fit the boy snuggly, in fact leaving nothing to the imagination. He could not help himself. Noah walked over to him and rubbed his hand across his chest. They smiled at one another and kissed each other lightly.

Noah asked, "Will you be my secret boyfriend?"

Jeremiah's heart erupted with gratitude. He placed his hand on the back of Noah's head and stared into his eyes, and he whispered, "If you want me to; it would be my honor."

Noah was ecstatic that he said yes, they sealed the deal with another kiss. Zeb shouted from downstairs startling the boys,

"Boys, hurry up; we have to get back to work." They both smiled at each other and raced out the door to the dining room downstairs.

The Confrontation 🌲

The boys finished their lunch while Rachel was in the kitchen trying to tidy up before heading back to the minister's house to finish cleaning. Zeb and David were on the front porch talking about the weather and how it was hotter outside than usual for the time of year.

Zeb asked David, "Do you think we should let the boys have the rest of the day off?"

David smiled back, "It sure looks like they earned it," he glanced toward the saw shop. Rachel emerged at the bottom of the stairs and called the boys to come downs; they had been upstairs relaxing for a bit before they had to return to the saw shop. Upon the sound of Rachel's voice, Noah and Jeremiah raced down the stairs.

Rachel yelled as they came down, "Hey, slow it down, you're gonna tear the house down!"

Noah bit his bottom lip chastised, and Jeremiah bumped into him halfway down the stairs. They stood for a moment, and Rachel yelled again, "Well, don't just stand there like a bump on a squash, move it."

Jeremiah pinched Noah's butt, and Noah yelped as he ran down the rest of the stairs. Jeremiah followed casually with a content smile on his face.

While Rachel locked the front door, Zeb and David greeted the boys, "Hi there, boys it seems you guys have done your fair share today, so David and I think you should have the rest of the day off."

Jeremiah was always so cool and smiled, thanking the men for their gift. Noah shouted, excitedly, "Really Pop?"

Zeb nodded with a smile and the two boys bolted from the porch like kids who had just been released from school for summer break. Rachel shouted to them, "Just be home by supper!"

They had made it halfway across the meadow when Jeremiah took Noah's hands; spinning around in a dance, and laughing until they fell down into the tall field grass. Noah laid on his back, gazing up at the sky momentarily, and Jeremiah laid on top of him. Jeremiah began tickling him, but no matter how much Noah protested, Jeremiah persisted. He paused gazing deep into Noah's eyes, and Noah smiled as he rubbed Jeremiah's chest exploratively through the open buttons on the shirt he had lent him.

Jeremiah whispered in a low masculine tone, "I could lay with you forever in this meadow."

Noah smiled again and closed his eyes; he sighed, "Me too, Jerry."

Jeremiah observed Noah's sun-kissed face momentarily as if it were a fine piece of art before bringing his lips to meet Noah's. Noah's lips parted slightly, and Jeremiah understood what he wanted.

Their breathing was soft and shallow as he gently slipped his tongue into Noah's hungry mouth, and Noah wrapped his lips around it, prompting Jeremiah's eyes to close from the pleasure of tasting his boy again. Their tongue's continued to dance. Their bodies pushing into each other like the wheat dancing in the wind.

They paused, and Jeremiah rolled over beside him, taking his hand as they caught their breath; he whispered, "Noah, there's something I need to tell you."

Noah turned to look at him as Jeremiah continued, "You know how you are supposed to like girls and marry them?"

Noah nodded in reply; his expression growing more concerned as Jeremiah continued to speak, "Well, I like boys the way we are supposed to like girls. My father knows and supports me even though in our world, it is forbidden."

Jeremiah sat up and turned away, trying to hide the tears he felt invading the corners of his eyes. Noah sat up too, placing his hand on Jeremiah's shoulder as he replied, "Yeah, but I can't believe the Lord will find anything wrong with two boys who love each other when there is so much hate in the world."

Jeremiah's heart sang; he turned to face Noah again and whimpered, "I don't want to lead you into temptation. If you feel like what we are is wrong."

He was trying to hold back the tears as the lump in his throat grew. Finally, he couldn't hold them anymore. With a shudder and a wave of tears, he cried out, "I don't ever want to hurt you."

Noah empathized with him and proceeded to wrap his arms tightly around Jeremiah; he spoke softly and calmly as the wind hissed across the meadow, "If loving you is wrong, then I don't ever want to be right again."

Their eyes met, and Noah traced the trails of Jeremiah's tears with his thumbs as he whined, "Please don't cry, Jerry; it hurts me so."

Jeremiah closed his eyes, and pressed his forehead to Noah's; he whispered, "I love you," expecting nothing in return.

Noah's eyes sprang open; his lips trembled as he replied, "I love you too, Jerry, so very much."

Jeremiah smiled; their lips met again as they slowly drifted back into the sea of golden grass and disappeared. The meadow was alive with joy. The wheat blew and rustled with applause. The birds soared high and sang their happy song of celebration. For all that was forbidden and wrong with their love, nothing else mattered because they had each other.

■■■■■■■■■■■■■■■■■■■■■■■■■■■■■■■■■■■

The weekend was fast approaching, and the boys spent the rest of the day walking and playing through the meadow and down by the creek. They snacked on apples from a tree and basked in the sunshine while making their plans for the weekend.

Back at David's house, Rachel had finished cleaning everything up and retired to the porch with some sun tea she had been brewing there all day. Zeb and David had managed to pack up all the old reverends paperwork and placed it neatly inside a closet in the back of the house. It had been a beautiful day, and everyone was ready to go home.

Zeb broke the silence, "How about you come over for dinner, no sense in cooking and messing up the kitchen for just you and Jeremiah."

David replied, "That sounds wonderful; I don't want to be a bother."

Rachel yelled from the porch, "Let It never be said that I let the Lord's man go hungry."

Zeb shook the man's hand, and they proceeded to their trucks. Noah and Jeremiah saw them coming down the road, and they both grabbed their shoes, racing them to get home. Everyone arrived at the same time, and David greeted Jeremiah with an inquisitive tone, "Have you boy's been behaving?"

Jeremiah grinned, "We tried."

Noah smiled at Jerry slyly as Zeb and Rachel got out of their truck. Rachel glanced over at the boys who were standing close to one another; she thought they were acting suspicious, and she wanted to get to the bottom of things.

Zeb was not as in tune as she was. He just thought let the boys be boys. She knew better with Noah. She knew he was impressionable like her, and she tried her best to protect him from himself and his own decisions. Addressing Jeremiah; she said, "Jeremiah, would you mind helping my husband Zeb load up you and your father's new furniture at the saw shop?"

The boy shook his head, yes. Noah glanced at him with a worried expression; he knew something was up with his mother. As Zeb and Jerry proceeded to the saw shop; she turned her attention to Noah, "Sweety, can you help me inside for a moment?"

Noah nodded, but he could not deny the sinking feeling he had in his stomach that something was wrong. Once they were inside, and the other guys were out of sight, she addressed him. "Noah, I know you have not ever met anyone you were as compatible with as Jeremiah, and you never show interest in any of the lovely girls, and you're eighteen."

Noah closed his eyes, wishing this moment would end. But. Rachel continued, "You should be spending more time with the girls in the community than with this boy."

Noah glared at her, defiantly, "I don't like the girls; I want to be with Jerry!"

Before he knew it, all of his emotions came out like water from a well pump. Finally, he understood his feelings as he shouted, "I want to be with Jerry, when I am with him my mind is still, when I am with him, my heart sings, When I am with him," his voice fell to a whisper, "I-I love him."

Rachel shouted, "How can you love someone you have only known for two days?"

Tears began falling from his eyes; he ran out the front door and dove from the front porch. Jeremiah saw that Noah was upset and ran down the hill from the saw shop frantically after him. Jerry knew something terrible had happened; he was nervous the entire time Zeb, and he was loading the new furniture into the truck. His heart could feel Noah's pain.

Like a wounded animal in the wild, Jeremiah had to get to him. Noah ran all the way down to the creek and collapsed on the shore. He was gasping for air in between sobs as he held his stomach tightly.

Jeremiah called for him, "Noah, Noah!"

He found his boy in a fetal position on the ground and dropped to his knees. Picking his body up and holding his body tightly up against his. Jeremiah whispered, "It's okay; I'm here!"

Noah's body was shaking from the force of the tears erupting from deep inside of him, and once he caught his breath, he began wiping his tears and rubbing his nose on Jeremiah's sleeve. He glanced up at Jeremiah's strong face and whispered, "Can we run away together?"

Jeremiah was shocked; he thought to himself, *what could have happened to make Noah this sad*, and he realized he needed to be careful with Noah; the boy's emotions were running wild, and Jerry knew he needed to rein Noah back in, but ignored the voices in his head telling him to stay cool.

He pulled Noah's face into his chest, and whispered, "If we need to, I will go with you anywhere, even to the end of the Earth if it would make you happy."

David was watching them from a distance he had chased after his son to see where they went. Naturally, he was worried and grief-stricken; he knew his son had a way of captivating people, and the last thing he needed was for little Noah to be another victim when they had to leave.

David had already known the position there in Elizabeth was temporary, but he didn't want to tell Jeremiah because moving around all the time was so hard on him. It was just easier to tell him of a transfer the night before they were scheduled to leave. Suddenly, he was afraid that not telling him this time could have been a mistake.

David decided that after Sunday service he would need to put in for an immediate transfer somewhere else. He couldn't risk waiting, and for the boys decide to run away or do something they couldn't get out of without significant repercussions.

Noah's mother Rachel was emotional inside as she prepared dinner; she had no intention of hurting Noah, and she understood that sometimes love can just happen; it had happened with her and Zeb. She knew she had to tell him, but she was not familiar with same-sex love; in fact, she had always considered it lust herself. Just a part of growing up, it seemed natural to "fall in love" with a friend whether they were male or female.

Zeb entered the house and asked in a panicked tone, "What happened?"

Rachel looked confused for a moment before telling him to sit down. They sat down at the dining room table, and with a sigh, she explained, "I think Noah may be confused; he likes boys the way he should like girls."

Zeb was lost in contemplation at what she had just told him. He replied, "What do you mean?"

Rachel looked frustrated with his response and quipped, "Zeb, I know you have to know."

Zeb lowered his head for a moment. "He never wanted anything to do with the girls from church."

Rachel shook her head in agreement. Zeb continued, "What are we going to do; You know the church's view on this situation?"

Rachel replied angrily, "We can't disown or shun our son, my little boy, y only child!"

Zeb took her hands, but their moment was interrupted by Reverend David, "My sincerest apologies, I didn't mean to overhear your conversation, but I can help you."

They both glanced at him, momentarily terrified that the reverend had overheard them. David asked, "Do you mind if I have a seat, what I am about to tell you is to be kept a secret, but I trust you."

Zeb replied, "Absolutely pastor, how can you help us with this?"

David continued, "My son Jeremiah is a very special guy. Like you, I noticed he wanted nothing to do with any of the girls we encountered at various places we have lived. One night shortly after my wife passed away, he came to me with a heavy heart and told me that he liked boys, the way he was supposed to like girls."

The good Reverend paused for a moment and looked back at them, "I could not have made it without him in my life after Sarah died. I believe that our Lord is a loving God, and he understands. It is not our job to judge anyone. I choose to walk in love and believe he would not want us to turn away our flesh and blood."

Rachel and Zeb shook their head in agreement. Rachel asked, "But Reverend, what will we say to people, we could be shunned for condoning this."

David continued, "My child, you are not condoning anything by loving your child. God gives us the free will to choose what paths in life we walk. Being gay is not a choice. They no more can choose who they love any more than you and I can. You should treat him no different, he is still the same boy you know and love. I warn you not to let anyone in the community know of our children's forbidden love."

Zeb replied, "What you are saying makes a lot of sense."

He turned to Rachel, "We need to let him know that we love him for who he is."

Rachel added, "We need to make sure he is careful not to get caught!"

David replied, "He is very safe with Jeremiah; the boy has great wisdom beyond his years."

Rachel sighed, "So, our sons are in love with one another?"

David nodded, and Rachel sighed.

The Runaways Vision ♥

Once Jeremiah had calmed Noah down, they both began walking back to the farmhouse. Noah was still upset and a little nervous. He knew by now his mother had told his father everything. They opened the door to find his parents and Jeremiah's dad in the dining room.

David addressed them, "Hi boy's, Have a seat for a minute; we need to talk to you."

David turned towards Zeb to let him speak. Noah was holding Jeremiah's hand under the table. "Boy's, Rachel has told me that you two are in more than just a friendship."

Noah's head dropped in despair. He had no idea what was coming next, but he was sure it could not be good. Jeremiah stared at Zeb solemnly; he was stroking Noah's hand reassuringly.

He nodded, "Yes, sir, it is true. We care a lot about each other."

David was observing their interactions carefully; he knew his son was a strong-willed person, and one wrong word could send him into a defiant rage.

Zeb continued, "It is okay for you boys to love each other, but we must request you keep any show of affection hidden from the public eye. We would rather have you remain in our lives, but until you have a place of your own. I request you respect the rules of this home."

It went better than Noah thought. He lifted his head to meet his father's gaze, "Dad, I can't change who I am."

Rachel interrupted, "Son, we love you, and although we do not understand these feelings you are having, we choose to walk in love."

David smiled; he wasn't sure what Noah's parents were going to say. He had prepared himself mentally to have to take in the boy, at least until he was a little older. Jeremiah replied respectfully to the man, "Thank you; I understand your stance on this. I can assure you that my intentions with your son are to nurture and teach him. I will protect him when he is with me."

Noah's parents were impressed with him. At least if Noah was with a man, it was a decent, honest man. Noah smiled at Jeremiah, and he winked back at him. He wanted so bad to kiss him right there, but he controlled his urge. Zeb finished the tense moment, "Well, boys, we have some furniture to deliver!"

He got up and patted David on the back, "You ready to go reverend?" and David replied, "Yes sir!"

The boys got up and began to follow the men out to the trucks. Rachel stopped them on the way, where Zeb could not hear. She spoke to Noah, "Noah, you are my baby, and I will always love you."

She took him by surprise and hugged him. He slowly lowered his head onto her shoulder. Next, she addressed Jeremiah, "Jeremiah, you, be sure to take care of my boy, like a good husband."

With a pat to his cheek, Jeremiah shook his head in reply, and the boys left the woman with her thoughts and chores.

David tossed Jeremiah the keys to their truck, "I will go with Zeb; why don't you guys take the drive and calm down."

Jeremiah grinned mischievously and cocked his head toward Noah to ride with him. Noah sprinted to the truck and hopped into the passenger's side. Jeremiah started driving toward his house, and Noah cozied up beside him in the pickup. Jeremiah wrapped his arm around Noah as young lovers do, and he whispered, "I have always dreamed of this moment."

Noah mumbled, "What do you mean?"

Jeremiah continued, "Driving my Dad's truck with my boyfriend by my side, breathing in the fresh country air."

Noah smiled and closed his eyes. He was exhausted from all the drama that had occurred. He was terrified that he might have not even had a home when it was all over. They arrived slowly to the parsonage. Jeremiah had never got the pleasure of watching Noah sleep, and he hated to wake him.

Once they had arrived; David walked over to the truck window and glanced inside. Jeremiah watched his father nervously as he peered in to see Noah sleeping up against him. He looked at the boy curiously and whispered, "Your mom used to do that when we were young."

Jeremiah smiled; he was relieved that his dad did not scold him after the warning Noah's parents had given them. He also remembered the warning his father had gave him when they first talked about his attractions to boys. But Jeremiah did not feel like he was leading Noah on. Noah was old enough to make his own choices and decisions.

As David went to the back of the truck to begin unloading furniture with Zeb, Jeremiah ran his fingers through Noah's hair and whispered, "Hey, buddy, we are at my house to unload furniture, wake up."

Noah stretched and yawned. He was looking around, trying to figure out what had happened. His eyes focused on Jerry, who was smiling at him. Jeremiah could not handle the amount of cuteness Noah was giving him.

Noah yawned again, "Oh, sure, that's right."

Jeremiah hopped out of the pickup and went around to open the door for Noah, who slid out like a lazy snake slithering down a tree. Jeremiah laughed, and Zeb peeked around the truck to see what the boys were laughing at. Zeb grinned, "Somebody's napping on the job!"

Noah stood to attention and apologized. His father shook his head; Noah always snapped to attention when his mom or dad said something; it was just a respectful mannerism built into his psyche. The boys met their dads at the back of the pickups and began unloading the new furniture Noah, and Zeb had made.

David pined over the craftsmanship, "This furniture is beautiful; I cannot tell you how grateful we are."

Zeb replied with pride, "You are most welcome friend, I'm glad you chose us to for the project."

It had been a long day for everyone, and the sun was setting in the distance. But now the cottage was clean and organized, thanks to Rachel's hard work. David and Jeremiah were both starting to feel more comfortable in the community and their home, especially now that they had something to sit on.

The weekend started tomorrow, which meant everyone would hopefully be able to get some rest. David needed to get to work on his first sermon and possibly his last there in Elizabeth. They all were sitting on the front porch of the little cottage, and as the sun began to tuck behind the horizon, they watched the lightning bugs and stars slowly began to make an appearance through the barren night sky.

Jeremiah and Noah were stealing glances at one another; their eyes were drunk with passion, and their bodies desperately longed to touch one another. The summer heat made their desires even greater. Jeremiah couldn't take the tension any longer and asked his father, "Can we run down to the creek and cool off for just a minute?"

Zeb shrugged, he didn't mind, and David replied, "Don't be long, we must get cleaned up and turn in for the night. We must make sure everything is ready for Sunday, and tomorrow, the community is having a potluck to welcome us."

Jeremiah nodded excitedly, and Noah jumped off the porch running across the meadow like a shot from a rifle. Jeremiah chasing him and laughing with delight.

It was magical; it was bliss; the lightning bugs dodging their bodies as they cut their way through the tall grass. Noah reached the creek bank first and leaned up against a tree to catch his breath. He had thought Jeremiah was way behind him.

Suddenly Jeremiah's lips met his sucking the remainder of his breath out of his body. Noah was shocked and aroused by the surprise; his fingertips pressing into Jeremiah's skin, as if he were holding on for his life. Jeremiah groaned in ecstasy at the applied pressure on his skin. Their tongues danced around one another's, and their breathing grew more labored with each passing second.

The smell of the creek and thick summer air filled their lungs like an ether.

Noah turned to place his head on Jerry's shoulder, and Jeremiah sunk his teeth into the boy's neck like a venomous snake. Noah's deep moans echoed from his body. He was terrified; he had never heard his body make such a sound before.

The sound was music to Jerry's ears and encouragement to keep munching away at Noah's neck. Noah gripped his hands tighter around Jeremiah's back; he felt himself submitting to Jeremiah's animal-like lust. He melted to the ground, and Jeremiah lowered himself on top of him. The bright light of the moon shined down on them with a haunting glow; it was tonight Noah felt like a man.

Their mouths searched for one another's again; their hips pressed tightly into each other's bodies desperately seeking release. Jeremiah lifted slightly and reached down to unbutton Noah's pants; slipping his hand into the boy's underwear. Noah purred like a kitten with every stroke of his hand. Nothing else mattered but the satisfaction he was feeling in this moment. Noah could smell his own body from the shirt he lent to Jeremiah earlier in the day. It was strangely erotic to encounter their essences mingled in the same garment. Jeremiah had been sweating heavy all day, and his musk invaded his nostrils like a drug, taking him ever higher.

■■■■■■■■■■■■■■■■■■■■■■■■■■■■■■■■■

Little did the boys know Jeremiah's father was still holding a secret from them. The long day had ended, and after eating the dinner, Rachel had packed for them, everyone was back at their homes getting ready for bed. Jeremiah was still wearing the shirt Noah had lent him. He laid in bed, inhaling the sweet aroma of him as the fresh night air blew across his body.

Noah was dreaming of Jerry as well; he gazed out the window from his bed, lost in his thoughts, how they longed to be sleeping beside one another in the same bed. Jeremiah's thoughts were interrupted by a quiet knock at the door. It was his father, David. The door slowly opened, and David called his name. Jeremiah hastily covered up to conceal his naked body and replied, "Yeah, Dad, what's wrong?"

David sat on the end of the bed and spoke softly, "Jerry, there is something I need to tell you."

Jeremiah had heard this song before, and he instantly was overwhelmed with anger. He gave his dad a chance to explain first. David sighed a ragged sigh, "Jerry, I have put in a request for us to transfer back to the city after Sunday."

Jeremiah jumped up from the bed. He was wearing a pair of shorts he slept in, and his shirt was open; he shouted, "How can you keep doing this to me, every time I find someone, every time I get used to the thought of being able to live a normal life without moving around all the time; you up and move us away!"

David's heart sank. He had never seen his son so emotional and angry; he held up his hand to try and stop Jeremiah and whispered, "Son, I think it is for the best. Think about Noah; he is too young to understand these new emotions you have introduced him to."

Jeremiah's eyes were aflame as he shouted, "You do not understand what we have!"

He collapsed in the floor holding his head in his hands. His body convulsing from the force of tears coming from his body, and he wailed, "I love him so much."

David sat down on the floor beside him and sighed, "I know son, but he is not like you. He doesn't know who he is as a man yet, and you would never be able to forgive yourself if you led him down the wrong path."

Jeremiah stood and shouted, "The heart wants what the heart wants; I knew I was gay when I was a little boy, I just didn't tell you until you found me kissing Zachariah."

David shook his head; he did not want to make Jeremiah angrier at him than he already was, but before he could say anything else Jeremiah jumped up and ran from the house letting the front door slam behind him. David jumped up, trying to catch him, shouting, "Jeremiah, son, please don't go!"

Jeremiah gazed back at him, tears streaming down his face, "I don't have to take this anymore; you can't take me away from him."

He lept from the front porch and began running through the meadow as fast as his body could take him. He was panting and desperate as he tripped and fell to the ground by the creek; he screamed out in pain as the thorns, and dry grass scratched his skin. As he glanced to assess the damage he had done, he noticed he was bleeding from his arms and legs. His head drifted back, and at that moment he wished he could die right there; at least he would forever be where he and Noah shared their most intimate moments, and as he gazed up at the starry night sky, he screamed, "God, why?" he exhaled and screamed again "Why?"

His body shook, but no more tears would come out, so he rolled over to his side and held his stomach, his pain now vocalizing in the form of dry heaves.

Back at the house, David sat on the front porch in tears and prayed, "God, what have I done, the only family I have left in this world. Please, God, let him come back to me. I can't go on in this life alone."

In the meadow, a vision appeared in before Jeremiah's eyes. It was a woman with a glow and beautiful long blonde hair. Jeremiah felt the pressure of a hand on his back and a voice whisper in his ear, "My child be not afraid. From the day you were born, I have watched you grow into the handsome man you are today. I have seen your darkest moments."

Jeremiah opened his eyes to behold the being who looked just like his mother. He stretched out his hand to hers, and the being smiled at him.

He whimpered, "Mama, is that you?"

She replied, "Yes, my son; you are my rainbow after the storm. Do as the good Lord says and be a light, finding the lost souls in this world."

Jeremiah shouted, "I just want to be with Noah; I don't want anything else from this world but him."

The woman touched his cheek, and he felt chills up and down his body as she continued, "Take care of your father for me; he only wants what is best for you, and he loves you more than anything in the world."

Suddenly the hovering light and being disappeared, leaving him in darkness; he stood staring up at the sky, all he could feel was emptiness, and he whispered, "Please don't go, mama. I love you so, and I need you." Overcome with emotion, his hands folded to his heart, and he fell to his knees in tears again.

■ ■

Back at the parsonage, David had hopped in his truck and drove frantically to Zeb and Rachel's house. They were the only people he knew in town, and it has been hours since Jeremiah had run away; he still had not returned. He lept from the truck and ran to the door pounding on it will his fists as he shouted, "Zeb, Rachel, Please, Help me!"

They both sprung from the bed, and Zeb ran downstairs to the door as Rachel pulled her housecoat together. Noah leaped from his bed, following his Dad down the stairs. Zeb held him back as he opened the front door, and David collapsed into Zeb's arms in tears, "Jeremiah ran away, we got into a fight after I told him we had to transfer back to the city, and he ran off to the meadow."

Noah's heart sank, and he tried to hold back tears as he shouted, "Which way did he go?"

David replied, "I'm not sure, son, he just ran across the meadow and disappeared in the woods."

Noah bolted out the front door. Rachel screaming from the top of the stairs, "Noah, no, it's dangerous at night."

Zeb added, "Noah, get back here now!"

Noah yelled back; tears streaming down his face, "No, we have to find him!"

The Decision

Noah tore through the meadow like a caged animal that had just been released; his screams echoing through the barren land like a siren, "Jerry, Jerry; It's Noah!"

He made his way down to the creek where he and Jeremiah had spent some of their most intimate moments; his mind was filled with confusion and sorrow. He could not bear to lose the only person he had ever shared such a close connection with. Noah paused to catch his breath, glancing up at the stars; he dropped to his knees to pray. "God, please let him be okay; please don't take him away from me." He began weeping as he whispered, "Jerry, I need you."

He heard a frail voice break through the silence, "I'm here my love."

It was Jeremiah; Noah crawled on his hands and knees to him and wrapped his arms around tightly around the boy he had come to love. He spoke through his tears,

"What happened; why did you run away?"

He laid down beside him and placed his hand on Jeremiah's face. "I can't make it through this life without you."

Jeremiah began crying again. Through his tears, he mumbled, "Dad had requested a transfer back to the city."

Noah screamed in agony and buried his face in Jeremiah's chest; he could feel the pieces of his broken heart dropping into his stomach, he just wanted to die right there next to the only boy he has ever loved.

Jeremiah pulled his body in close to his, and they held in silence, Noah nuzzling his chest and body like when they first met down by the creek, trying to memorize every detail of Jeremiah's physique with his hands.

Jeremiah whispered, "I hurt myself when I fell."

Noah opened his eyes to observe the damage. Jeremiah was bleeding from his leg where the thorns had slashed his flesh open. Noah panicked and jumped to his feet. He ripped off his shirt. His beautiful young body highlighted by the moonbeams shining down. He dipped it in the creek and began rubbing the blood off his wound.

Jeremiah cried out in pain, "Ah, it stings so much."

Noah was trying not to cry, seeing him in pain broke his heart so much.

He whispered, "Don't worry, I will take care of you. I need you."

A tear slid down his cheek, and he leaned down to kiss Jeremiah. "I – I Love you."

Jeremiah opened his eyes, and he whispered, "What did you say?"

Noah froze and gazed into his eyes with an expression Jeremiah had never seen. It was pure and innocent and full of truth. He whispered again, "I love you, Jeremiah, and I can't imagine growing older without you."

With his hand, he made half a heart, and Jeremiah lifted his hand with the other half instinctively. Noah whimpered, "You complete my heart," and they placed their foreheads against one another's.

Their parents had been watching from just out of sight. Rachel was in tears, and Zeb had a look of deep worry on his face. David looked at them with tears in his eyes, and Zeb whispered to him, "Reverend, we have a problem."

David replied solemnly, "I know."

Rachel was touched by their sweet forbidden love, and she whispered to Zeb. "They love each other; they really do."

Jeremiah spotted them out of the corner of his eye, and his eyes filled with rage. He struggled to his feet, and Noah offered his hand to help Jerry up.

David jumped and spoke to him, "Please don't run son, we only want to help you."

Jeremiah pushed Noah protectively behind him. "I am done with you, taking away my choices."

Rachel stepped forward, and the men let her. She stepped lightly toward him. His muscles bulging with youthful rage, and his eyes filled with anger. She spoke gently, "Sweetheart, I know you are hurting but try to listen to someone who was just as angry as you when I was young."

She continued, "No one is going to separate you and Noah. I can see how much he cares for you and if your father needs to go. You can stay here with him."

His body relaxed, and he exhaled a sigh of relief. Rachael's expression remained unchanged as she continued to speak; gentle but firm, "Now calm down so we can figure this out together."

Noah stepped from behind him placing his hand on Jeremiah's shoulder reassuringly. Jeremiah tried to walk, but he was limping and almost fell; Noah caught him. For such a small guy, Noah was strong as an ox. Zeb walked over and propped the boy upon his shoulder, and they helped him back to their farmhouse. When they reached the porch, they all sat down, and David began speaking, "Son, I don't want to lose you. You are a man and can make your own decisions. I cannot stop you from doing anything you want to do, and I understand that you want a life of your own."

He began weeping, "I just want to be a part of it. I could not live with myself if I could never see you again."

Jeremiah was listening carefully to the words as he said them. After a long pause, he responded, "Then why can't we just stay, here in Indiana?"

David replied, while wiping the tears from his eyes. "Son, I need you to understand that if you need to stay here with Noah, I understand. But, I have a long life left to live, and I need to continue with the Lord's good work. There are so many young people who were just like you that need to know they are loved; You taught me that. Don't you see he has a special plan for you, to show the young boys like Noah who feel frightened of the emotions that what they are feeling is normal."

What his father was saying resonated with him; he glanced over at Noah, his heart aching to be with him, and he whined like a puppy as his head dropped.

Zeb and Rachel were both watching the conversation with deep concern, and Zeb spoke to Jeremiah. "Son, I cannot thank you

enough for bringing our boy out of his shell.
Before you showed up, he barely spoke at
all."

Rachel shook her head in agreement.
She added, "Whatever decision you decide
to make, you have a home here with us until
you can make one for yourself."

Noah smiled; he never knew how
supportive his parents could be until now.
He knew in his heart that many boys did not
have it so lucky. Noah squeezed Jerry's
hand and spoke softly, "We should get some
sleep so that we can spend as much time
together as possible."

His voice cracked a little with what
he said next. He gazed deep into Jeremiah's
weary eyes and said, "Whatever you decide
to do, I will understand." A lone tear fell
down his face.

Jeremiah thought he was there to
help Noah, but Noah was actually helping
him come to terms about who he was going
to be as a man. David smiled at the boy's
wisdom. His parents were shocked by what
he was saying. He had somehow over this
short time become a man, and the little boy

they knew was gone; He was making unselfish and difficult decisions for the better of someone else, not just for himself, and they found that very honorable.

David interrupted the moment and directed his attention toward Jeremiah. "I hope you will forgive me for anything I said that hurt you. Let's go home and get some rest so we can greet the town, and you can spend the day with Noah tomorrow."

Noah smiled; he was comforted by the reverend acknowledging him. Noah wasn't sure at this point what decision Jeremiah would make, but just in case. He wanted to spend as much time with this wonderful boy as he could in the event they were going to be separated for a greater good. Turning his attention to his mom and dad; he mumbled: "Can Jeremiah spend the night here?"

They glanced at David, "What do you think, reverend?"

He replied with a nod, "That would be fine with me" His tone turned stern for a moment, "As long as you two don't run away or do something crazy."

Rachel addressed his concern, "Pastor you do not need to worry about that, nothing gets past these eagle eyes."

The woman pointed at her eyes and then pointed at the boys. Making sure to make deep eye contact with them. Zeb shook his head in agreement with her statement as she pointed at him next. He knew his wife well, and he knew when she was dead serious. Noah hopped up, and Jeremiah wrapped his arm around him for support, "Let's go get cleaned up!"

Rachel interrupted, "One at a time; I will run a bath. We will put some Epson salt in there; it should help with the pain and swelling."

David patted Jeremiah on the back and spoke, "I love you, son!"

Jeremiah had finally reached a state of calm. Just being near Noah was soothing the rabid beast inside of him. He replied to his father with a weary sigh, "I love you too, Dad."

David shook Zeb's hand and walked wearily to his truck. The drive back to the parsonage seemed to take forever. His mind filled with thoughts of whether he should stay there in town or whether he should go back to the city where he felt he could make a bigger difference.

Although the little town of Elizabeth had seemed to offer more problems than he ever could have imagined. His heart longed to be back near the people he knew. He and Jeremiah have had difficult moments in the past, but none of them so bad to make him run away from him. Jeremiah was a strong, free-thinking man and being out in the country had brought out the wild side of his heart. He knew what he had to do. He just prayed he was making the right decision.

A New Day ☀

     The next morning the boys awoke next to each other in bed. Noah was sleeping quietly with his hand on Jeremiah's naked chest. He smiled and closed his eyes; he never wanted this moment to end. He just wanted to lay there with him forever. In the back of his mind, Jeremiah remembered the vision he had received the previous night; seeing his mother again brought back so many memories and emotions. She was such a loving and accepting woman.

     He knew his dad always wanted him to pursue life as a reverend. His youth was the only thing hindering him. He was a deeply spiritual person and spent every night in prayer and reading his devotions as a good Christian boy should. He also remembered what Noah's father had told him. About how he brought Noah out of his shell and for the first time, was interacting and speaking to other people. Everyone could tell, even Jeremiah, that he was more confident and secure in himself. Just by the way, he walked and carried himself.

His mind wandered in many different directions. Now he was enjoying the peace he was feeling being with Noah. How satisfying and "hot" it was being in Noah's bed and room. He was even wearing a pair of Noah's pajamas, which were slightly too small. It didn't bother him though.

It was a special kind of erotic to be in the clothing that touched his sweet Noah's skin. He bit down on his lip, trying to suppress the growing urge he was now feeling inside his pants. Noah smiled and reached his hand over to touch it. Jeremiah moaned with want feeling his soft hand caressing it.

Noah whispered, "You appear to be awake."

Noah giggled with delight as Jeremiah pushed his hips forward with want to meet his hand. Jeremiah groaned again, "Hey, that's not fair; I was trying to be good."

Noah hummed with delight and spoke again, "Sometimes being bad, feels so good."

Jeremiah could not take it anymore. He pulled Noah up on top of him, and they began kissing passionately. They both knew they only had a brief moment of privacy before Noah's mother came up the stairs to wake them up, even though it was Saturday. There were still lots of chores to be done on the farm.

David was up with the sunrise as he always was; he had been in prayer and reading his bible all morning, searching for confirmation that he was making the right decision. There was no way to tell for sure until the choice had been made. He had learned from his past, that even if it was the wrong choice. The Lord sorted things out for good in the end. He did not want to spoil the festivities for the town, so he had made the decision not to say anything to the congregation until the end of Sunday service.

All though they would be disappointed, he knew they would be able to move on with their lives easier if he left now. He did not want to prolong things. He knew from his last congregation how hard it was to separate himself after being somewhere for a very long time. He had spent most of Jeremiah's growing up years in the big city. He had thought moving out to the country would be safer for a boy just coming into manhood. The city could be dangerous for someone, even if they weren't looking to get into mischief. But, he never thought Jeremiah would meet someone as sweet as Noah.

His innocence was precisely what Jeremiah was looking for, and David knew his son well. He was a kind-hearted boy, and he knew someone like Noah would steal his heart away. David was sad; he did not know what Jeremiah would choose. If he stayed with Noah, it would mean long periods of time where they would not see each other. But if he went with him, he wondered if Jeremiah would later resent him. David did not want him to choose because of him. He was a man now and whatever decision he made, needed to be well thought out and based on where he thinks he could best be a productive adult. That was the ultimate goal of any parent. He just wanted to see his son happy.

Zeb was sitting out on the front porch drinking his coffee with Rachel. They had also been up since sunrise, discussing the events that had transpired last night. Zeb was not the type to express his emotions, but Rachel could tell the whole series of events had shaken him. Seeing his son caring so much for another man. It was all so unconventional. He had never seen such passion and love; it moved him. Rachel was worried about Noah. If Jeremiah left, what would Noah do?

She told Zeb, "I can't bear to see our little boy in pain."

Zeb shook his head in agreement and responded with sympathy. "That's the problem, dear; he's not a little boy anymore. He's a grown man and has to live with the choices he makes."

Rachel sighed. "I guess I better get the boys up. I have lots of cooking and things to do for the potluck at the church."

Zeb pinched her butt as she walked by and she smacked his hand. "For shame," she squealed and blushed as she modestly placed her hands behind her.

He grinned like a possum momentarily before replying to her concerns, "I think we both agree that no matter what choice the boys make, we just need to love them without judgment. Besides, if Jeremiah does stay here, we can always use another set of hands for all the work that needs to be done around here."

Rachel shook her head in agreement and opened the screen door. She shouted as she started up the stairs, "Boy's time to get up, we have to get chores done and get Jerry to the church."

They were both still exhausted, not just from last nights events, but they had just finished an intense session of lovemaking in Noah's bed. The boys jumped to attention; they did not want Noah's mother to catch them snuggled up so intimately. Jeremiah was supposed to be sleeping on the floor in a sleeping bag. They both knew that wasn't going to happen; they had been longing for this moment ever since they met.

The Potluck

Everyone from the little town had gathered at the church for the big potluck to welcome David and Jeremiah. David looked out the window to see the little dirt parking lot full of buggies and old pickup trucks. It was a beautiful day, and the Indiana summer sun was shining brightly.

Ladies and their daughters were setting up the picnic tables with pretty tablecloths and enough food that could feed an army. David felt guilty that everyone had gone through so much trouble, and he was not even going to stay. He hoped and prayed that the town folk would be forgiving. There were lots of children playing in the meadow. The sweet song of laughter and joy filled the air. When the people of Elizabeth got together to fellowship with one another, it was like a celebration.

Back at the farmhouse, the boys were getting ready. Noah was looking sharp in his handmade slacks and a bright flannel shirt. He was wearing his Amish hat, and Jeremiah smiled at him. It was all a bit traditional for him. Growing up in the city, his manner of dress was more casual than the people here in Elizabeth.

Rachel knocked on the door and came in with a gift for Jeremiah. The surprise took him back a little. Rachel sat on the end of the bed and slid the simple box tied with string into his lap. Noah bit his bottom lip nervously, he already knew about what was inside, and he hoped Jeremiah loved it. They were going to give it to him at church tomorrow, but Rachel figured now was a perfect time since he had spent the night and would not have a chance to go back home and change before the potluck supper.

Jeremiah questioned, "What is this?"

Rachel smiled with a sweet smile, and Noah pleaded, "Open it, open it!"

He carefully untied the string and opened the lid on the gift box. It was a beautiful outfit. A white button-up shirt and black slacks. Underneath was a shiny pair of black loafers. Jeremiah gazed gratefully into the woman's eyes. "Thank you so much. I don't know how I can ever repay you."

Rachel shook her head and took the boys hand. "You do not owe me a thing, just making my boy happy is a gift in itself."

Noah wrapped his arms around her from behind and kissed her on the cheek.

He turned to Jeremiah, "Mama had been working for the past few nights making them just for you."

Jeremiah studdered, "B-But, how did you know what size I wore?"

Noah smiled, I checked while you were in the bath to make sure, but she made them one size bigger than my clothes. We knew the shirt I lent you fit a bit too snug, so she made them just a little bigger."

Rachel cheered him on, "Go to the bath and try them on; we can't wait to see!"

Jeremiah hopped up from his chair with excitement and made his way down to the bath to change. He did not want to give Noah back the shirt he had loaned him. It was so special to him and made him feel close to the boy he loved so much. Rachel and Noah waited patiently in the bedroom for him to emerge.

He met his mom's gaze and smiled, "Thank you so much for everything you have done for Jerry and me."

She hugged him and replied, "I would do anything to see you happy."

She moved the hair from his eyes. "You need a haircut son."

Noah shook his head and pushed his hair back. It frizzed up in a messy pile on top of his head. She smiled and shook her head. Their moment was interrupted by a quiet knock at the door. It was Jeremiah. Noah jumped up and down, excitedly at how well it fit.

"Way to go, Mom," he cheered.

The woman placed both hands on each side of her face and smiled. She was so happy with how well it fit Jeremiah and how handsome he looked. He stood with his hands in his pockets with a shy smile. Noah's heart flip-flopped. His white shirt tucked neatly into his pants and his new loafers shining brightly.

Noah ran to his closet, "You're only missing one thing to look authentic."

He grabbed a pair of thin black leather suspenders and an old hat of his. He handed the hat to Jeremiah, who looked at it skeptically. It wasn't really his style, but he understood that the people here dressed differently than in the city. Noah was a blur as he hooked the suspenders to the back of his slacks and latched them onto the waistband of his pants. The tension of the straps pulling his pants tightly up, showing off his perfect muscular butt, which made Noah blush. He stared at it for a moment, and Rachel caught him.

Pulling him back; she quipped, "Okay, that's enough, son. Come back around here."

In the nearby mirror, Jeremiah slid the hat on and ran his fingers around the brim. Then, he turned to them and grinned. "So, how do I look?"

Rachel smiled and shook her head, "Very distinguished."

Noah cleared his throat, "Most handsome boy in town."

Jeremiah smiled and winked at him with approval. Rachel stood and hugged him; she patted his cheek with a content smile. "Hurry down, boys; we have to get to the dinner as soon as possible."

Once she had left and closed the door behind her, Noah bolted from across the room and placed his hand behind Jeremiah's neck, kissing him so hard, it practically sucked the air from his lungs.

Jeremiah gasped and asked him, "What was that for?"

Noah smiled and whispered, "I love you so much; you're my big strong Amish man now."

Jeremiah rolled his eyes. "Amish, not quite the look I usually go for; how about blue jeans and a normal shirt?"

Jeremiah ran his finger around the collar of the shirt. Noah shook his head at the sarcasm. "I think you look very handsome."

Jeremiah replied, "Well, as long as you think so, then I am happy" They kissed again, and Jeremiah opened the door motioning for Noah to go first. Noah gestured femininely and put his hand over his chest, "Why I do declare sir, will you be my escort for this evening?"

Jeremiah curled his arm out like a proper gentleman, and they headed down the stairs. They made sure to look like appropriate gentlemen when they exited out to the porch. They both knew they would get in trouble for acting foolish, and neither of them wanted anything to spoil the wonderful time they were having together.

Besides, in the back of Noah's mind, he still did not know what Jeremiah would choose to do. He just wanted to live in the moment, because at any moment, they might be separated. It broke his heart and made him sick to his stomach every time he thought about it. Jeremiah's mind was a storm of emotions. He loved being with Noah so much. But the vision he had, made him more aware that if he stayed in Elizabeth; His father would be left alone, and he could not do that to him.

At times he wondered if he could convince his father David to stay. He knew in his heart though that once his dad had decided, it was very rare for him to change his mind. The whole ride over to the church,

Jeremiah could not take his eyes off Noah. He was unaware this time; Jerry was watching him. He was running his hand through the wind lost in his thoughts. His eyes were closed, and he was basking in the warm sunlight on the back of the pickup. Jeremiah had a sinking feeling in the pit of his stomach. He had been to many functions like this before. He was reminded that he would need to put on a show and flatter the young ladies that would be here.

He closed his eyes too, trying to relax before they arrived. He despised the fact they would be pining over him and touching him. It would feel like cheating now that Noah was his boyfriend. What was he going to do?

The Last Supper

They had just arrived at the dinner. There were way more people there than any of them could have thought. David was already mingling and getting to know the town people. He waved at the boys who were sitting on the back of the pickup truck bed. Jeremiah hopped out first and took Noah's hand to help him down. He had to resist the urge to grab Noah's waist and sit him down on the ground. He treated Noah with the same class and respect a gentleman would his girlfriend.

As they turned around, all the local girls were smiling and conversing among themselves. They were hungrier than a wolf after a long cold winter, and Noah knew it. He wasn't prepared for the show Jeremiah was going to have to put on to satisfy the town folks suspicions of a "gay boy" in town. Noah was very selfish and jealous by nature, and he instantly became defensive. He wished there was a way to mark Jerry, saying essentially the boy is mine. But there was nothing he could do as he watched nearly every teenage girl in the county make their way over to the well-dressed boy.

They giggled and squealed with glee as they all introduced themselves, pulling him away with them to the picnic tables. One offered to fix him a plate, another offering him a soda pop. It was sickening. Rachel came up behind Noah and whispered, "Son, are you okay, you are shaking!"

Noah's face was red with anger. Rachel covered her mouth and whispered, "My God, they ambushed him!"

Noah screamed in agony as he turned to his mother, "He's mine."

His mother tried to catch him as he bolted away; his body spinning around, and he staggered trying to catch his balance. He held his stomach as he ran into the meadow. He felt like he was going to throw up.

Rachel screamed for Zeb and turned toward the direction he ran to "Noah, Noah, Come back!" She pointed and screamed, reaching the direction he ran.

Zeb hollered up at Jeremiah who had already seen the commotion out the corner of his eye. "Jerry, Noah's gone, he took off toward the woods."

Everyone was watching the commotion with shock and panic. They weren't sure what had even happened. Jeremiah tore his way from the town girls. The buttons of his shirt ripping open. Rachel was crying and sitting on the back of the truck bed as several of the ladies she knew came over to comfort her. Jeremiah ran like a cheetah after his prey in an African desert. Zeb had stopped a few hundred feet back. He was just too old to catch Noah.

Jeremiah yelled at him, "Don't worry sir, I will get him."

Jeremiah growled and grunted as he ran faster and faster. He could see Noah collapsed by their tree near the creek. They both ran away to the same place every time, the place where they first met. It was a sacred oasis, a holy place for the two of them.

Jeremiah yelled at the boy, "What the hell is wrong with you, why the hell did you run away like that?"

Noah lifted his head with tears streaming down his face. "How dare you question me?"

Jeremiah realized his tone had been way sharper than he intended. He knew how fragile Noah was and what he said could have done irreversible damage.

Jeremiah placed his hand on Noah's back and whispered, "I'm so sorry, Noah!" Noah screamed in agony and crawled on the ground like an animal trying to escape being captured and screamed, "Don't you dare touch me!"

Jeremiah froze, and his face was shocked by the way Noah was acting; he quipped, "I don't understand, Noah, please tell me, what did I do?"

Noah shot a scornful look his way, and his tone cut to the bone, "You mean to tell me you don't know."

Jeremiah threw his hands in the air, "I have no idea, baby."

Noah's body began shaking, and he waved his hand at Jeremiah as if to tell him to leave him alone. He covered his face with his other arm. Jeremiah sat down on the ground, tears streaming down his face; he pleaded, "Please, Noah, please come back to me. I can't lose you!"

Noah lifted his head and said coldly, "I never want to see you again."

Jeremiah's heart shattered like a baseball through glass. Everything went dark in his mind, and all sense of emotion left him. He was numb. His whole world ended with six words. He slowly got up from the ground. He turned to look at him one more time, trying to capture the boys face in his mind forever. As he walked back to the potluck, Zeb and Rachel ran up to him, even more, concerned since Noah was not with him.

Rachel screamed, "Jerry, where is he, did you not find him?" She turned to Zeb, "Oh God Zeb did he fall in the creek?"

Zeb silenced her with a Shh and pulled her into his body to console her.

Jeremiah stood silently, unable to speak, with tears streaming down his face.

Zeb shouted, "Son, what happened, where is Noah?"

Jeremiah sucked in a breath of air and moaned in despair, "He never wants to see me again."

Jeremiah covered his eyes with his hand and ran toward his house. David separated himself from a group of men he had been chatting with, and he ran in after Jeremiah. The door to his room had just slammed closed before he made it. David paused and leaned against the wall trying to catch his breath as he spoke to Jeremiah through the closed door. "Son, what happened, where did Noah go?"

Jeremiah screamed in pain and covered his face with a pillow. He was sick of all the questions. He just wanted to be alone and die. He answered reluctantly, "Noah ran away; he never wants to see me again." Each time he said the words, it felt like a knife plunging deeper into his heart.

David sighed; he knew something terrible would happen eventually. He had forgotten all about the potluck at this point. He suddenly remembered the deal they had made long ago, about flattering the town girls and being discreet about who he was.

Zeb called from the front door, "Take your time reverend. We have everything under control out here."

He was relieved to have such a good friend in Zeb. He knew so well how to calm any tense situation. Rachel was doing her part to diffuse the confusion as well. She explained to the town ladies that Noah and Jerry were friends and they were simply having a disagreement about something. It wasn't the full truth. She had told herself, later she would ask the Lord's forgiveness for her dishonesty, but right now she needed to smooth everything over with the town people. The men of the community were not concerned with whatever had happened, much to Zeb's relief. They were still discussing the normal topics, Hunting, Fishing, and Farming.

While Rachel and Zeb were tending to the potluck and explaining to the town people what had happened, David sat by Jeremiah's door listening to his agonizing cries. He just wanted to be near him, even if it wasn't in the same room. David was a wonderful father and pastor, even if he did not know what to say to comfort, someone. Just his presence was soothing. Jerry knew his dad was right outside the door, and after almost an hour, he mumbled, "It's unlocked dad."

He was facing the wall hugging the shirt Noah had lent him. David spoke softly as he attempted to lighten the situation, "Wished I would have known that an hour ago, that floor is hard."

He placed his hand on Jeremiah back and rubbed it gently as he took a seat at the end of the bed, "Just let it out son, I know it hurts."

Jeremiah squeezed his eyes even tighter while David kept encouraging him, "It's okay son; I am right here. You don't have to say anything."

Jeremiah felt empty as he laid there, staring at the wall. The only image in his mind was Noah. He could not feel anything at this point but a void where his heart used to beat. David stayed by his side until he fell asleep and then went back outside.

The worried town girls were waiting in a group by the house. One little blonde girl about seventeen asked David, "Will Jeremiah be rejoining us?"

David smiled at the little girl. "I'm afraid not my dear, all the moving and work has him not feeling well."

She bowed her head in disappointment and replied, "Tell him we will be praying for him."

David replied kindly, "I will, my dear. He will appreciate that."

The Aftermath

Noah wasn't doing any better. He was angry with himself that he let such a minor thing bother him. In his mind, he knew Jeremiah loved him, and those girls meant nothing to him. He didn't even know them. They were just doing what girls do. He was the first eligible boy to move to town since they were all children. As he walked home, the words he spoke played in his mind like a broken record. He regretted everything he said. The image of Jeremiah's face burned in his mind: The hurt in his eyes, the pained expression on his face.

He prayed to himself, "Please God, help me, my heart aches to be with him again and pretend this horrible thing did not happen."

Once he arrived at the farmhouse, he realized his Mom and Dad were still not back from the potluck. He knew the front door was locked, but all he wanted to do was climb into bed and erase this pain. He walked up the hill to the saw shop and leaned against the wall inside, memories flashing through his mind of their first intimate moment there; He closed his eyes as tears began to well up inside of him again, he moaned, there was nowhere he could go to escape the emptiness he felt.

Noah became more reclusive than ever before. Neither of the boys felt they would ever be the same again. It was like one half of his heart had died. He didn't even get out of bed to go to church on Sunday. Rachel and Zeb only checked on him a few times to make sure he was okay even though they knew he wasn't.

Jeremiah was not in church either; he was at home, packing his things. His decision had been made for him. David's heart ached for his son; he knew something was different, and he wondered if Jeremiah would ever be right again. He had not spoken since last night. Jeremiah hugged the shirt Noah had given him tightly again. He wept into it as his nose filled with Noah's essence. He would never trade the moments he and Noah shared for anything in the world.

He dropped to his knees in desperation and prayed, "Dear God, if I could just have one more chance to see him. If I could just hear his voice one more time."

David heard his plea and came into the bedroom, wrapping his arms around his son. Jeremiah whimpered, "Dad, it hurts so much."

David whispered as they rocked back and forth in the floor; Jeremiah head on his chest, "I know son, I'm here for you."

David finally separated from him and went to lock the suitcase. He reached for the shirt Jeremiah was holding, and he recoiled. Jeremiah shook his head and yelled, "No, please, I need it," He held it close to him like a baby and whimpered.

David closed the suitcase and loaded it into the truck. Afterward, he came back inside and mumbled, "Son, it's time to go back home."

Jeremiah stood in the empty room. He would never forget his sweet Noah, but he couldn't bear the pain anymore. He folded the shirt neatly and laid it gently at the end of the bed.

He kissed it and whispered, "Goodbye, my love, I will never forget you."

It was early Monday morning, and Noah had managed to pull himself together enough to help his dad in the woodshop. He had refused breakfast and instead sat out on the front porch staring out across the meadow. The light morning breeze making the wheat and wildflowers dance.

The dust kicked up on the main road; he saw David's truck from a distance coming up the dirt road that passed the farmhouse. Zeb watched the boy and finally spoke to him. "Son, if you love him, this is your only chance. Go to him!"

Noah dropped the piece of wood he was whittling from his hand and looked into his father's eyes. Zeb smiled at him, "Son if there is one thing I have learned in this life. If something is meant to be, then It will be. But you will never know if you don't live. No matter what, love conquers all and can find a way."

Jeremiah closed his tear-filled eyes as the truck neared the farmhouse. He could not bear to look. Suddenly across the meadow, he saw a figure moving through the wheat, and they heard screaming.

It was Noah screaming, "Wait; please wait. Please don't go!"

Noah was growing tired as he neared the road. David began slowing down the truck, and Noah collapsed in the middle of the road as the truck disappeared.

Noah screamed up to the heavens, "God, No!"

He began pounding the dirt road with his fists, and He whispered, "I was too late."

He laid down on the ground, his hands over his eyes, as the sun's rays disappeared behind the clouds. He just wanted to die. In his mind, he could not silence his thoughts. He would never have the chance to say he was sorry. He would give anything to see Jerry; his beautiful Jeremiah one more time: to kiss his soft full lips, to feel his strong arms wrapped around his little body, to taste his tongue in his mouth, to run playfully through the meadow, until they both crashed down on top of one another. Never again to swim and play by the creek they loved so much…

Never again.

The Reunion 🏠

Noah thought he was hearing things when a voice echoed from across the meadow. "Noah, please don't leave Noah. I'm coming!"

He opened his eyes enough to see a figure running toward him, and as it got closer, he realized it was Jeremiah with his suitcase. He screamed again, "Please wait for me!"

Noah stood to his feet in disbelief. His feet started moving to the end of the driveway until he was running again. Jeremiah stopped at the corner of the driveway where the meadow met the road and sat his suitcase on the ground. He held his arms wide open as he continued running toward Noah. Their bodies made contact so hard Jeremiah knocked Noah down in the tall grass landing on top of him.

They stared into each other's eyes for a moment, and Jeremiah pushed his lips tightly against Noah's. The wind blew across the meadow, and the clouds shifted, opening the sky. Sunlight enveloping around their two bodies as their hearts merged again. It was like being reborn. There had never been a more beautiful moment in all of time when Jeremiah whispered, "I could not leave without kissing you one more time."

Jeremiah cupped Noah's cheek in his hand and winked at him. Noah pushed his forehead into Jeremiah's. "I could not let you leave without saying, I'm sorry for everything I said to you."

He began to cry, "I just want to be with you forever, and seeing someone else doting on you hurt me so bad."

Jeremiah shook his head and mumbled, "No one else can ever mean anything to me, I would have rather never been born if it meant I couldn't have met you." Noah erupted in tears, and Jeremiah held his head into his chest, "I'm here, baby, and I'm never going to leave you."

When David slowed down the truck, he could see the pain Jeremiah was in; he kept looking back over his shoulder like he had forgotten something important. David had stopped and pulled to the side of the field, "Son, I can't bear to go on living my life, knowing you aren't happy. You belong with Noah; you grew up before my eyes, and now I have to let you go and be your own man."

Jeremiah began to shake from the force of tears flowing from his body. "I just want to be with him. Dad, I'm so sorry, I didn't even get a chance to explain what happened and tell him goodbye."

It was then David realized the shirt Jeremiah had been holding onto was gone. He asked, "Where is Noah's shirt, did you forget it?"

Jeremiah spoke through the tears, "I left it at the parsonage. I couldn't take him with me."

David reached across him and opened the truck door; he shouted, "Go to him, son!"

Jeremiah wiped the tears from his eyes and gazed into his father's eyes. David spoke again, "Please, son, hurry, he will think we're gone!"

David grabbed the boy by the neck and kissed his forehead and wrapped his arms tightly around him one last time. They separated, and Jeremiah panicked as he rushed to get out of his seatbelt and grab his suitcase from the truck bed.

David shouted, "I will be in touch; go to him!"

Jeremiah stood as the dirt cloud dissipated around him. He had heard Noah stop running. Jeremiah ripped down the road as fast as his legs could take him. He screamed, "Please don't let him go, God!"

"Please, please, please," with each stomp of his foot into the gravel road, it echoed. He paused at the end of the meadow. It was then he saw him; his beautiful Noah standing, staring off into nothing. Just like he always did. Oh, how he longed for one more taste of Forbidden Ecstasy.

EPILOGUE

Twenty years had passed since the day Noah and Jeremiah had reunited. Jeremiah's father lived the rest of his life as a minister in the city where he and Jeremiah had lived before moving to Elizabeth. He had finally grown tired of the world and wanted to go home to be with his sweet wife. Just like reverend Sigafoos in Elizabeth, he had passed away silently in his sleep one night.

Everyone assumed from a heart attack; the good reverend loved life and food. He had gained quite a substantial amount of weight in those last few years. The day after his funeral, Noah and Jeremiah had brought the good reverends ashes back to Elizabeth and set them free across the meadow on Noah's family property.

Jeremiah's dad had always felt, from dirt we were created and to dirt we should return. They had taken over Noah's fathers business when he had become too old to take care of it anymore. They continued living on the land Noah's family had always owned and built a little cabin by the creek where they had their first intimate moments. It was their sanctuary.

Even at forty-two, Noah still loved seeing Jeremiah's tight butt in his blue jeans. Jeremiah was chopping wood in the front yard, and Noah was propped up on the front porch lost in his thoughts as per usual. Jeremiah winked at him and stretched, exaggerating the form of his butt. He always could feel Noah's eyes on him, and it made him feel so good. Noah still looked the same way he did at nineteen skinny and athletic with his copper red hair and wispy little beard.

The sun was now casting the last rays of light across the meadow, and Jeremiah sauntered up to the front porch of their cabin and kissed Noah on the cheek. "Is dinner ready baby, I'm starved."

Noah grinned and shook his head. "It's been ready for ten minutes, but you were busy showing your ass."

Jeremiah stared at Noah with a shocked expression as he held the screen door open, and Noah smiled back at him like he always did; he whispered, "I was enjoying the show, so it's okay." Jeremiah winked at him, and they kissed one another as they stepped inside the cabin.

Rachel and Zeb both lived well into their eighties. Their love lasting up until the very end. When Rachel passed away, Zeb followed her just a few short weeks later, they left the farm and all the land to Noah and Jeremiah.

Noah's mother used to walk down to the cabin every morning to wake the boys up and bid them good morning. Neither of them were very good housekeepers. They were quite the burly men who enjoyed hiking and camping when they weren't working.

Regardless of what they were doing or where they were, their wishes came true; everything they ever wanted what was forbidden, came to fruition in due time.

THE END

ABOUT THE AUTHOR

Daniel Elijah Sanderfer is a retired Hospitality Manager who currently resides in Southern Indiana with his husband, William.

Originally from the Blue Ridge Mountain region of Virginia, he moved to Indiana to be closer to his then fiance. They have been married for two years and together for fifteen total years.

He was always interested in writing even from a young age and was featured in a few poetry collections as a teen. When he is not writing, he is caretaker, as his husband is disabled and requires full-time care. He enjoys going to antique stores and in the summer weekend long yard sales.

He currently writes LGBT fiction with a positive direction as he feels too many love stories experience tragedy. He likes to highlight the stories that survived — the couples who fought to stay together and the families that do accept them.

FOR MORE GREAT STORIES BY DANIEL
ELIJAH SANDERFER PLEASE FRIEND HIM ON
FACEBOOK AND JOIN HIS FAN GROUP
SANDERFER'S SOCIALITES.

HE CAN ALSO BE FOUND ON QUEER
ROMANCE INK, AND HIS NOVELLAS CAN BE
PURCHASED AT AMAZON.COM

Made in the USA
Coppell, TX
24 November 2020